To Jo, my English sister, who touched my
life and filled it with colour.

And to all of those who still haven't
found their hidden talents.

G.M.

First published by Macmillan Children's Books an imprint of Macmillan Publishers LTD 2013.
Distributed in the United States by NorthSouth Books Inc., New York 10016.

Library of Congress Cataloging-in-Publication Data is available.
Printed in Shenzhen Wing King Tong Paper Products Company
Limited. Shenzhen, Guangdong, China, November 2013..
ISBN: 978-0-7358-4163-5 (trade edition)
1 3 5 7 9 • 10 8 6 4 2
www.northsouth.com

THE CROCODILE WHO DIDN'T LIKE WATER

Gemma Merino

North South

Once upon a time, there was a little crocodile.

And this little crocodile didn't like water.

He longed to play with his brothers and sisters.

But they were far too busy with swim club.
And this little crocodile didn't like swim club.

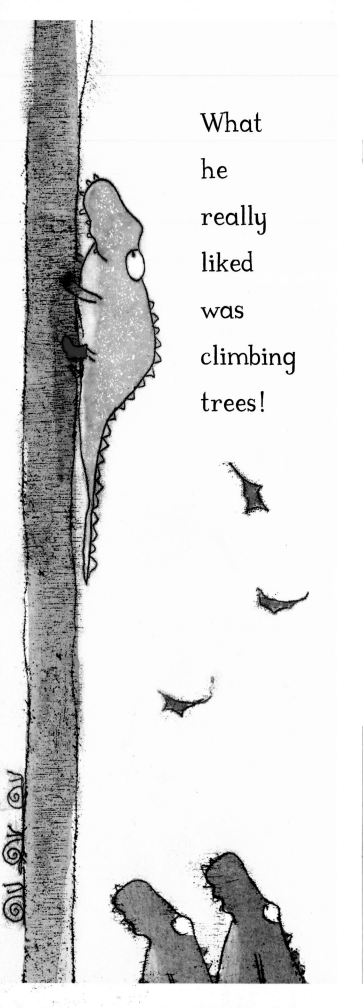

What
he
really
liked
was
climbing
trees!

But nobody else did.

It was lonely having nobody to play with.
So the little crocodile made a decision.

He had saved up his money from the tooth fairy,
and he knew exactly what to buy with it.

The next afternoon he took his
new swim ring over to the water.
Today he would play with his
brothers and sisters!

But he couldn't play ball.

Or swim underwater.

And although climbing the ladder was fun,

he

just

didn't

want

to

J

U

M

P.

But he didn't want to be alone.

So he decided to try, one last time. . . .

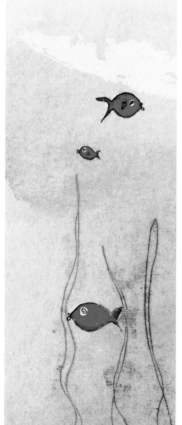

One,

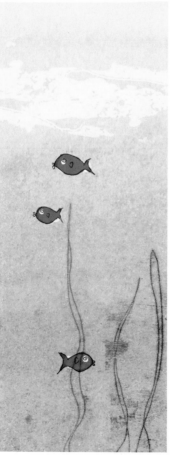

twooo,

two
and
a
half,

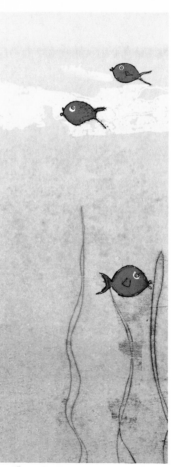

THREEEEEE!

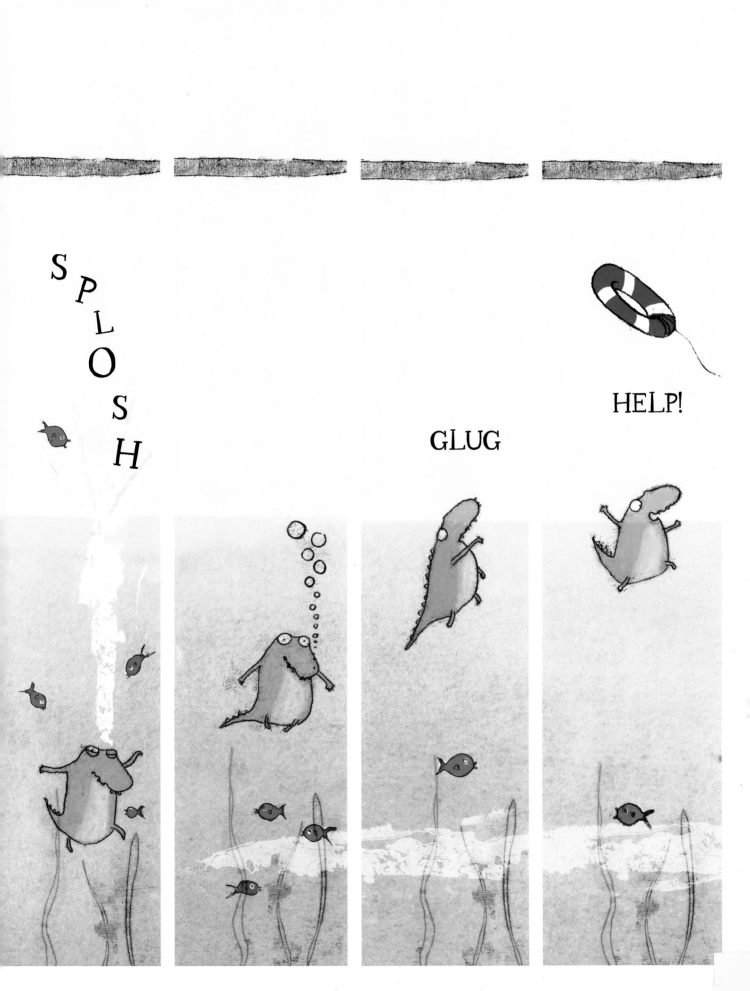

This little crocodile
definitely hated water.
It was cold,
it was wet,
and it was embarrassing.

But then something
strange happened.

His nose began to tickle,

and the tickle grew,

and grew,

and grew,

until . . .

AAAACH

This little crocodile
didn't like water,
because he wasn't
a crocodile at all!

He was a DRAGON.

And this little dragon
wasn't born to swim.

He was born to
breathe fire.

He was born to fly!